DRESSES, DREAMS AND BEADWOOD LEAVES

Julia Taylor Ebel

High Country Publishers

INGALLS PUBLISHING GROUP, INC

Boone, NC

2009

High Country Publishers
INGALLS PUBLISHING GROUP, INC.
197 New Market Center #135
Boone, NC 28607

www.ingallspublishinggroup.com

Book and cover design by Ann Thompson Nemcosky

Library of Congress Cataloging-in-Publication Data
Ebel, Julia Taylor.
    Dresses, dreams and beadwood leaves / Julia Taylor
Ebel.
        p. cm.
    ISBN 978-1-932158-85-4
  1. Appalachian Region--Poetry. 2. Appalachian Region--
Social life and customs--Poetry. 3. Mountain life--Appala-
chian Region--Poetry. I. Title.
    PS3605.B44D74 2009
    811'.6--dc22

                                        2008037992

First Printing, January 2009

In memory of Mom and Lois,
mothers who sewed,

and for Jeanette
and all the daughters who have dreamed

Acknowledgments

My gratitude goes to those who have enlightened me on herbs in the mountains: to the Hardin sisters who told me about gathering beadwood leaves, to Kenneth and Chris Wilcox, who told me about the business of buying roots and herbs, and to Tony and Sandy Hayes who answered more questions. Thanks to David Cuzzo, whose research on root and herb gathering affirmed my observations and pointed me where I wanted to go.

Thanks to those who talked with me about their own herb gathering: to Dennis Wood who took me on a wet but wonderful hike through hills and hollows to see nature's treasure trove of herbs; to Orville Hicks, whom I met over my questions about herb gathering—but that was just the beginning.

Thanks to Betty Lou Wells, who remembers the healing ways of her grandmother, Chaney Brown Hardin, herbal wise woman. Thanks to all who have believed in this story, including my sister-in-law Jeanette Curtis and my friends Pat Koehler and Carole Weatherford. As always, thanks to my husband, Alan, for his support—technical and otherwise.

Thanks to Bob and Barbara Ingalls of Ingalls Publishing Group/High Country Publishers for seeing purpose in my words and for taking me into their circle of writers.

DRESSES, DREAMS AND BEADWOOD LEAVES

Eastern Hemlock

Winter, 1948

I watched snow
burying the mountains,
blanketing roads,
and hiding woodpiles,
but Mama'd planned ahead
and canned food
from summer's harvest.

Today,
I warmed
and read
by the woodstove
as she trudged through snow
and toted a sack of food
to Miss Minnie
up in the hollow.

Mama came home
cold,
empty handed,
and plumb worn out
but singing.

Beadwood (Witch Hazel)

Waiting for Spring

March came
with icy wind
and lingering snow.
I shiver
as Will, Davy and I wait
for the school bus.
My fingers ache
inside thin gloves,
and my bare legs sting
in the biting wind,
sting from my ankles
all the way up
to my knees.

Cows huddle
in the field nearby.

Davy teases,
"If you'd stand
in a cow patty,
your feet would be warm."

"You're funny," I say,
but I know he's right.
No telling
what would happen
if I showed up at school
smelling
like a cow patty.

Poke Salad

Mama's going to have to stretch
those last jars of food
in the cellar
if growing season
doesn't come soon.

I dream of roaming free
in warm spring sun
and gathering
new leaves
for poke salad.

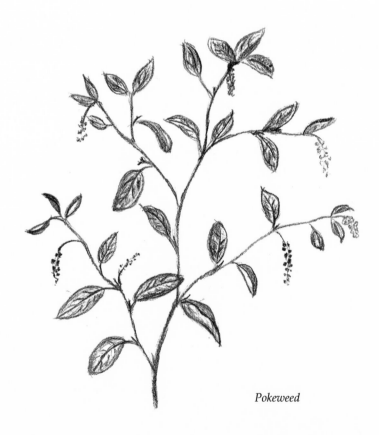

Pokeweed

Spring Growth

Come spring,
my legs grew
like field grass
after April rain,
grew
till Mama
patched a hole in my dress
then gave me
a needle and thread
and told me
to let the hem out.

Now I look
at the faded crease
in my dress
and try to iron it out,
but it won't go.

Mirror

The girl in the mirror
has grown tall,
leaving knees
shining
below
the pale dress
that hides
her dreams.

Sometimes
I wonder
if I fade away
like old calico colors,
washed until
they're barely seen.

Unnoticed

I know the answer
and raise my hand,
but the teacher
picks someone else.

At lunch, Mary Jane
and Lucy
and Marcella
talk and talk
about goings-on in town,
as if fancy goings-on in town
are all that matter,
but those things
aren't for me.
Suddenly,
I feel left out
when Marcella looks at me
and says,
"You're so quiet, Rosa May."

Of course, I'm quiet,
and I can't say anything now
for the knot
of wounded pride
in my throat,
so I just try to smile.

Nurse

I'm thinking
about the nurse
who came to school
back in winter.
We had chicken pox
all over the school,
so the county sent her
to check on us.

She spoke to me
in a soft voice,
so kind
and yet so sure of herself.
Her warm hand
touched my shoulder.

I wonder
if she noticed
when I touched
her ironed white dress.

I wonder
if I could learn
to be a nurse
with a soft voice,
a gentle hand.
and an ironed white dress.

Summer

School's out today.
Summer starts.
Just in time
'cause this dress
is just about
worn to threads—
this old calico dress
that Mama made
from leftover feed sacks.

Soon
Mama'll tend the garden—
     planting,
     hoeing,
     picking,
     canning.
No new dress
for me
till summer's end
when canning
is done.

Dreams

I wish
Mama and Daddy had money
for store-bought dresses
every now and then.
Mary Jane,
Lucy
and Marcella
always
have pretty dresses—
store-bought.
Come school time again,
I want to wear a new dress too—
store-bought.

Maybe then,
the whispers
will stop.

Shame

Thoughts
keep going back
to a day
last May.
As I sat at my desk,
I saw eyes
peek back at me.
Mary Jane's eyes.
Lucy's too.
I heard whispers.
"Rosa May's dress....
Her mama and daddy
can't do any better
or else don't care."

How dare they say that!
They don't even know
Mama and Daddy.
I'll bet their mamas
don't even know how
to stitch a seam
or make a buttonhole.

My cheeks
burned with anger
and with shame.
I looked down
at my history book
and tried to read,
but the words
made no sense
that day.

My eyes settled
on a lapful
of threadbare dress,
still short,
with its patch
and old hemline
shining
in a faded streak.

I closed my eyes
and wished
I could stay home
from school
to help Daddy
with planting.

I knew better
than to cry at school
in front of
girls from town,
but walking home
alone,
I let tears fall
and wash
my secret hurt
away.

Catalog

Daddy left
the Sears, Roebuck catalog
on the table
last night.

I've been looking at it
ever since,
looking
at dresses,

wishing one
would come
in a box
for me —

    Rosa May Liddy
    Route 1
    Deep Gap, North Carolina

Last summer
nothing mattered
but running along
behind Will and Davy,

begging them
to let me play ball.
"My little tomboy,"
Daddy called me.

This year
I have my own plans.

Help Wanted

Mrs. Marlow wants a girl
to do house chores.
"I can iron and sweep,"
I tell Mama.
"I can earn money
for school clothes."
But Mama says, "No,"
and looks away.

That night,
Mama and Daddy talk.
"No daughter of mine
is going to clean
someone else's dirt,"
Daddy storms.

If only I could talk
about girls at school
and shame
and dreams
and dresses.

Sometimes
Daddy and Mama
are too proud
for their own good,
but I ache
to earn
my own
pride.

Night Stitches

Somehow Mama sees
the pretty
in common things,
so she saves old sugar sacks,
flour sacks,
feed sacks.
Every one has a use,
Mama says.
At night
Mama cuts
and stitches,
turns sacks
into clothes
and quilts.

Nobody sees the bloomers
Mama makes
to go under my dresses.
But they see the dresses.

Shoes

Rocks on the road
poke through
my worn-out shoe soles.
Mama can make a dress
but she can't
make
shoes.

Barefoot

In summer
I walk
across the yard
barefoot
then wade
in the creek,
washing the day's dust
off my toes,
letting that dirt
float down the creek
to who
   knows
      where.

No need
for shoes
in summer.

On My Own

Last year
I helped Mama
gather beadwood leaves.
She tucked
the money we earned
into her money jar
to buy school shoes
for Will and Davy
and me.

I can't work for Mrs. Marlow,
but I'll gather my own leaves
and earn my own money,
to buy my own dress.

Beadwood

The Business of Medicine

Mr. Wilcox
in town
buys herbs.
Dried leaves,
roots,
and bark--
that's his business.
There's money
in medicine,
so he sells the leaves I pick
to big companies
that make remedies
for people
all over the world.

Maybe clover
and catnip I pick
in the hollow
will go
all the way to New York.
Maybe
my beadwood leaves
will go to Germany
or Italy
or France.
Maybe.

Ready for Gathering

Mama stitched
a tough fertilizer sack
into a pouch
for beadwood leaves
I'd gather.
And from a flour sack,
she made me a glove
with three fingers
and a lined palm.

I set out
through the woods
with a glove on my hand
and a pouch
tied round my waist.

Beadwood Dollars

I slide my hand
along a beadwood branch.
Leaves fall
into my pouch.
I imagine each leaf
is a dollar bill.
Five,
   ten,
      fifteen.
I'd have enough money
to buy fancy dresses
for Mama and me both.
I'd buy Daddy
a suit
and a necktie
and a fine felt hat.

Store Bought

It's not
that a dress Mama makes
isn't pretty,
but something
about store-bought clothes
tells a girl
she's got a place
in this world.

Gathering

All week
I packed beadwood leaves
into the pouch
Mama made.
Mr. Wilcox
will pay me
six cents a pound —
dried.
That's thirty cents more
I'll have,
thirty cents of a dress.

Balm of Gilead buds,
goldenseal,
galax —
every leaf I pick
draws me closer
to my dream.

Galax

Store Window

I saw the dress
in the window
at Mr. Kelsey's store.
It's blue
like the autumn sky
with tucks down the front
and white buttons too.

Lady's Slipper

A patch of lady's slippers
is growing
in the woods.
Lady's slipper roots
bring a good price,
but I can't
bring myself
to dig up something
so pretty.

Pink Lady's Slipper

Remedy

Here in summer
Mama took sick--
a cough
that wore her down
and wouldn't quit.
Aunt Sadie,
who heals folks
all over the county,
said to give her
mullein and cherry bark.
Instead of selling herbs,
I'm brewing them
into tea
for Mama.

Mama sips
and nods
her thanks.

Mr. Wilcox
will have to wait.

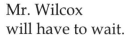

Mullein

Dreams Revealed

I told Mama
I'd like to be a nurse
and bring healing
to these forgotten hills.

"You'd be a fine nurse,"
she said
and smiled.

"I'll wear a white dress,"
I told her,
"clean and starched,
ironed real smooth."

I told her about
the store-bought dress
I wanted
for school too.
She nodded.
I could see old dreams
in her eyes.

Mama told me
how she'd dreamed
of a big farmhouse
made of smooth stones
and how she'd
bought a dress
when my sister Betty Jean
got married.

I didn't dare
tell her
about the whispers.

Queen Anne's Lace

Down the road
a patch
of Queen Anne's lace
caught my eye,
so I picked a few stems
and put them in a jar.
Mama smiled.

A little pretty
goes
a long way.

Queen Anne's Lace

Beans and Biscuits

Mama's getting better —
slowly.
"Sit back down,"
I tell her.
I put wood on the stove
to cook beans
and bake biscuits
for Daddy,
Will, and Davy —
hungry menfolk
coming in
from farm work.

Drying

Feed sacks
laid open
in the summer air
make drying sheets
for beadwood leaves.

I stir
and wait,
stir
and wait,
until
the leaves crackle
between my fingers.

In Town

This afternoon
Daddy let me
ride to town
with him.
There on the main street
Mary Jane strutted along
in a dress
just like the one
in Mr. Kelsey's window.
Daddy went to the farm store,
but I ran up
to Mr. Kelsey's store.
The dress
was gone.

Daddy's Feed Sacks

Daddy
came back
from the farm store
with five sacks
of feed,
all bagged
in the same blue calico.

"Thought that flowered print
would make a pretty dress,"
he said.

Mama says
Daddy's got an eye
for good fabric.
He's careful
to pick good sacks,
   no holes,
   no rips,
   no stains,
enough good cotton
to sew
into a dress.

Debt

I wash dishes
as Daddy sits at the table
adding up
his credit bills
for farm supplies,
for flour and sugar,
and for Mama's medicine—
bills he'll pay
when cash crops come in.

"The almanac's promising
a wet month,"
he tells Mama.

Mold and rot
ruin bean and potato crops—
same as no rain.

Farming
is steady work
but risky business.

Secret

I tiptoe
to the cupboard
and slip
most
of my beadwood earnings
into the nearly empty
money jar.
Mama still needs medicine.

In the field
I gather clover blossoms.
Then I turn toward the woods
to fill a sack
with beadwood leaves.

Come school time,
I'll have
a store-bought dress—
but not the one
I had my heart
set on.

Red Clover

Ginseng

There's ginseng
up in the hollow —
enough ginseng
to fill a money jar.

Daddy says wait
until September frost
to dig ginseng root,
till seeds
are ready to drop —
seeds to grow
come spring.

I wish I had
that ginseng
now,
but ginseng's scarce enough
without wasting seeds.
Daddy's right.
I'll wait.

Ginseng

Not Enough

In August,
roots and herbs
add up
but not enough
to buy a dress
and the shoes I need too.
So I choose.

I open the catalog
to the page
with the red plaid dress.
Mama measures me
and helps me
choose the right size.
"You're getting to be
a young lady,"
she says.

Mama watches me
address the envelope
to Sears, Roebuck
and lick the stamp.

And she watches me skip
to the mailbox
with my order in hand.

Waiting

One week,
two weeks,
three weeks—
how long will it take
to get my package?
I watch each day
for the mail.

Celebration

Daddy comes in
grinning.
"Got a good price on beans today.
Enough to buy flour,
sugar,
and cocoa powder."

At supper,
we celebrate
with chocolate gravy
on biscuits.

Beadwood

The Package

Just in time —
the package came,
wrapped in brown paper,
but the package held
no plaid dress,
bright as autumn trees.

I'd changed my mind
and ordered shoes
to wear with the dress
Mama and I made,
   blue calico
   with white buttons,
   tucks,
   and grosgrain ribbon trim —
prettier than the one
at Mr. Kelsey's store.

Someday soon
I'll order
that plaid dress.

Someday
I'll wear white.

WITCH HAZEL
BEADWOOD

Hamamelis virginiana Linnaeus

Witch Hazel is a deciduous native shrub or small tree, growing 20 to 30 feet in height.

Leaves are asymmetrical and shallowly lobed, growing 3 to 5 inches long and 2 to 3 inches wide.

Flowers are small and yellow, with four wispy ribbon-like petals. Flowers appear along branches from October into December and remain after yellow leaves drop.

The term "beadwood," used in some regions, comes from the hard bead-like seed capsule with four curved points at the tip. When dry, seeds explode from the capsule.

Witch Hazel grows commonly in moist, rich hardwood forests of Southern Appalachia, but its habitat extends through most of the eastern United States.

An extract from Witch Hazel leaves, bark, and twigs has long been used medicinally as a mild astringent.

ROOT AND HERB GATHERING
IN SOUTHERN APPALACHIA

The Mountain Environment

Through the early and mid 1900s, people who lived in the Southern Appalachian Mountains knew the land. Mountains limited travel. Families stayed close to home. These Appalachian people learned to live from the land in order to survive. Rocky hills limited farming, but a small farm could provide food for a family. Families traded extra produce for needed supplies.

Traditional Home Uses of Roots and Herbs

For centuries, people have used native plants as food sources. People also have eased their pain and soothed illnesses with teas and salves made from roots and herbs. Mountain people knew these herbal remedies. They respected local "herb doctors," who shared knowledge of plants' healing powers. As trained doctors and modern medicine became more available in the mid 1900s, people used herbal remedies less.

Roots and Herbs	Traditional Use
blackberry	nausea, diarrhea
cherry (fruit and bark)	cough
dandelion	blood cleanser, rheumatism
goldenseal	antibiotic
jewel weed	poison ivy
mullein	cough, asthma, earache
purple coneflower (Echinacea)	immunity
plantain	bee stings and snake bite
yarrow	cold, flu, bleeding

Gathering

Many Appalachian people learned to recognize the native plants. They spoke of these plants with common names, like beadwood (witch hazel), life plant, and turkey corn. They gathered roots and herbs and passed along knowledge of wild plants to their children. By the age of six or seven, children could help with root and herb gathering.

Mountain people first gathered roots and herbs for personal use. Later, they sold these plant materials. Families bought school clothes and shoes for the children with profits from root and herb gathering. Native plants provided the primary income for some families. Money from the sale of roots and herbs not only bought clothing but also helped pay electrical bills and property taxes.

Plant Materials Gathered	
Plant Part	Season Gathered
buds	spring
fruit	summer
leaves (herbs)	summer
roots	summer and autumn
bark	spring and summer

Marketing Roots and Herbs

Root and herb gatherers have collected hundreds of plants for sale. Many plants are still gathered. Wild cherries and cherry bark make cough remedies. Witch hazel makes a mild antiseptic. Wintergreen, or teaberry, provides flavor. Ginseng, now scarce in the Appalachian Mountains, has been highly valued in Asia as a cure-all. Even poison oak and ragweed pollen are gathered and sold for medicinal use.

Most roots, herbs, and fruits are dried before they are sold to make medicines. Other natural materials are sold fresh for floral uses. Shiny galax leaves and log moss are still sought for sale to floral markets.

Weight of Gathered Plants		
Plant	Fresh	Dried
witch hazel leaves	4 pounds	1 pound
ginseng root	3 ½ pounds	1 pound
(Enough fresh ginseng to fill a grocery bag will fill a paper lunch bag when dried.)		

Buyers of Roots and Herbs

Wilcox Drug Company in Boone, North Carolina, was a primary supplier of native herbs. The Wilcox family operated the business--from 1900 until 1994. The Wilcoxes bought a variety of dried roots, leaves, flowers, and berries from local gatherers. In turn, Wilcox Drug Company sold these plant materials to companies that made medicine and other products.

Wilcox Drug Company purchased over two hundred different plant items from root and herb gatherers. Prices paid for these roots and herbs varied greatly. Ginseng always topped the price list. Wilcox paid $9.00 per pound for dried ginseng in 1948. The price of ginseng peaked in the mid 1990s at around $550.00 per pound. Much ginseng went to Central Asia.

Prices per Pound Paid by Wilcox Drug Company (1900-1985) and Wilcox Natural Products (1985-2000)						
Herb Prices:	**1936**	**1948**	**1958**	**1973**	**1983**	**1999**
balm of Gilead buds	.10	.70	.25	.70		
catnip leaves	.09	.10	.38	.55		$1.25
cherry fruit	.10	.15	.15	.30	.50	
cherry bark		.15	.02-.07	.06-.16		
ginseng			$9.00		$115.00 -200.00	
mullein		.02	.02			.60
poke root	.02	.07	.03	.08	.50	
red clover blossoms		.25				
wintergreen		.20	.15	.50		
witch hazel (beadwood)	.01+	.06	.09	.40	.35	$1.25
witch hazel bark		.03	.05	.16		$1.00

Today

In years past, numerous companies bought natural materials from root and herb gatherers. While the number of buyers has dwindled, root and herb gathering continues in Southern Appalachia and in other regions across the county.

Responsible Gathering

By following basic guidelines for collecting roots and herbs, gatherers can collect plants safely without threatening the future of the plant species.

1. Get permission from landowners before gathering.

2. Gather no more than 40% of the plants in an area.

3. Do not gather where a species is scarce.

4. Do not gather where chemicals or contaminants may affect the plants (near industries, by roadsides, near or downstream from livestock).

5. Take only what is needed and have a plan for its use.

6. Dig roots after seeds form.

7. Scatter seeds near the original plant so new plants can grow.

8. Unless roots are needed, leave roots undisturbed.

9. Leave small plants so they can mature.

10. Avoid damaging other plants or scarring the land.

For Further Thought

A study guide and book discussion starters are available
free of charge on the author's website page for
Dresses, Dreams and Beadwood Leaves.
www.juliaebel.com

Welcome to books from
High Country Publishers of
INGALLS PUBLISHING GROUP, INC.

For more information on books and ordering and
links to authors' websites, visit our main website at:
www.ingallspublishinggroup.com
www.highcountrypublishers.com

High Country Publishers

INGALLS PUBLISHING GROUP, INC

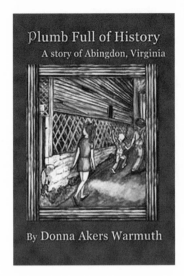

Plumb Full of History:
A Story of Abingdon, Virginia
by Donna Akers Warmuth
ISBN 1-932158-78-2 $9.95

Abingdon, Virginia's Plumb Alley Day frames this story of two children discovering much more than the history of their grandmother's hometown. Addie, a self-concious thirteen-year-old and Owen, an enthusiastic nine, feel very differently about the prospect of accompanying Gram, their volunteer tour guide, as she experiences this familiar celebration of Abingdon's history. By the end of the day, however, both have come to understand much more about their place in their family and in the history of the region.

"Readers young and old will find a treasure trove of Virginia history in this lovingly-crafted tale of Abingdon past and present."
— Sharyn McCrumb, New York Times Best-selling author of *The Song Catcher*

"Donna Warmuth is a wonderful writer, so entertaining that the story really takes over and history comes alive on the page before us. Great reading for all ages."
— Lee Smith, award-winning author of *The Last Girls*

"What a delightful, informative book! Though intended for middle grade readers, Plumb Full of History: A Story of Abingdon, Virginia will be enjoyed by both youth and adults."
— Klell B. Napps, of the Historical Society of Washington County, Virginia

The Secret of the Lonely Grave

by Albert A. Bell, Jr.

ISBN 978-1-932158-79-3 $8.95

*Winner of the **Evelyn Thurman Young Reader Award 2007**.*

Steve (a baseball freak) and Kendra (a sassy Sherlock Holmes wannabe) were friends "before they knew they were not supposed to be." They discover flowers on the "lonely grave," an isolated headstone in the corner of an old graveyard they pass walking home from the school bus. Their investigation leads them through the history of Kentucky, the Civil War, slavery and the Underground Railroad and discovers secrets even their parents would prefer remain hidden.

"Masterpiece for 9-11 year olds. The reader will not be able to set down this gripping and fast-paced tale as the plot twists, turns and literally tunnels through a history of Kentucky, the Civil War, slavery and the Underground Railroad. As a parent, teacher and writer, I give this book an enthusiastic thumbs-up; it's a must read!"
— Karen Hoenecke, author of 30 children's books

"What a fantastic book!" — Book Review Cafe

"...an entertaining mystery that even adults could enjoy. It has some memorable characters, as well as lessons about why hatred and bigotry are wrong...while they learn, kids are treated to a great can't put it down mystery." — My Shelf.com

"What a super story. ...excellent example of contemporary mystery ... characters are believable and sassy ... excellent story line, great characters, and issues with bullying, family values, and a strong sense of friendship."
— Donna Morse, **Front Street Reviews**